THE MAVERICK MOON

illustrated by Walter Wright

STAR WARS™

THE MAVERICK MOON

Random House 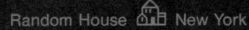 New York

In another time, in a faraway galaxy, there lived a young man named Luke Skywalker. He was a student at the New Academy for Space Pilots, and already he was one of the best young pilots in the solar system.

Luke and his classmates, the Planetary Pioneers, were training for a special mission. They were going to fly young men and women—the smartest and strongest and most talented—to uninhabited planets. There they would help build new colonies, founded on peace, justice, and good will toward their fellow members of the galaxy.

One morning Luke raced toward the Academy at breakneck speed. His good friend Princess Leia Organa was coming to visit the Academy. Luke wanted to be there when she arrived so he could show her some of the Pioneers' exciting plans.

When Luke reached the Academy, he hopped out of his landspeeder. Some of his friends waved or called good morning. All of them smiled. They knew why Luke was in such a hurry. Princess Leia had arrived. Although she was one of the youngest members of the intergalactic government, she was well known to everyone.

Luke proudly showed Princess Leia around the Academy. He told her about the work of the Planetary Pioneers. "Some of us will be building homes and schools and power stations," he said. "Right now we are planning to use our powerful Zukonium rays in the power stations. Instead of being used for war and destruction, Zukonium will provide energy for our colonies."

"It sounds terrific, Luke," said Leia.

Suddenly a screaming siren pierced the orderly hum of the Academy hallways. That siren meant *emergency!*

Luke and Leia raced to the office of General Oleson, Luke's favorite instructor. "What's wrong?" asked Luke.

The general quickly explained the emergency. A small moon from a nearby system had been blasted out of its orbit. No one knew how or why. The moon was surrounded by a powerful magnetic field. None of the Academy's sensors could pierce it. Now the maverick moon was on a collision course—traveling at well beyond light-speed—and it was headed their way! "We'll be meeting in the conference room in five minutes," said General Oleson. "I'd like you to be there, Luke."

Luke and Leia hurried to the conference room.

An enormous monitor in the conference room was tracking the course of the maverick moon. Its path was obvious to everyone. In just a few hours, the maverick moon would collide with them, blowing the Academy—and indeed the whole planet—to smithereens!

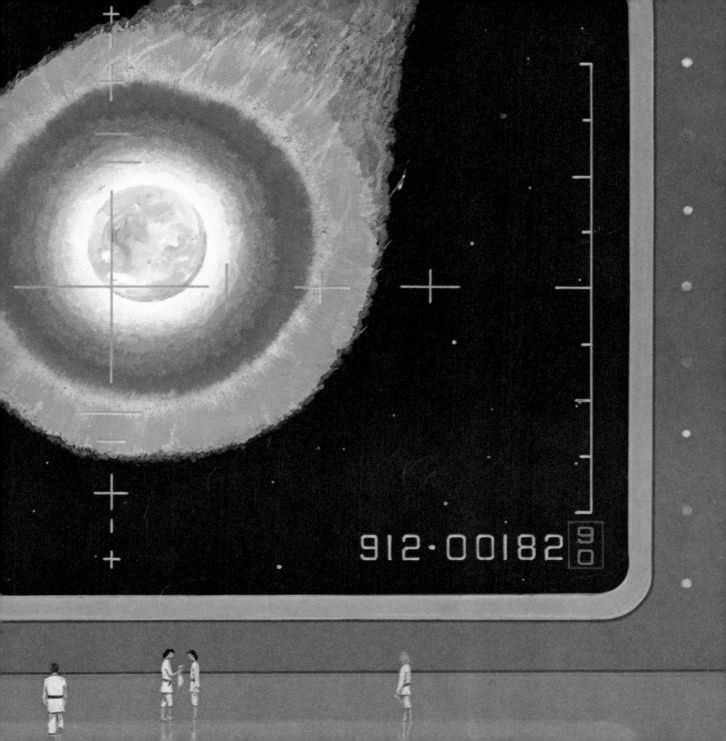

912·00182 9 0

"We don't have time to evacuate the planet," said General Oleson. "Besides, we don't have enough spaceships to take everyone to safety."

"We still have our old fighter planes!" said Luke. "And we can use the power we've developed with our Zukonium rays to blow that maverick moon right off the star map!"

General Oleson looked thoughtful. "Even if those old ships will still fly, you couldn't get close enough to blast that moon. The magnetic field is impossible to penetrate."

"I'd like to try it," said Luke.

"It's our only hope," said Leia.

"Go ahead and try it, Luke," said General Oleson.

Luke went to find his friends See
Threepio and Artoo Detoo. These
extraordinary robots had helped
him before, and he knew they were
in excellent working condition.

"I'll get Artoo ready for the
flight, sir," said Threepio.

Little Artoo's lights blinked on
and off as he beeped and whistled
his eagerness to help Luke.

Luke's X-wing fighter plane was brought to the hangar. Artoo was lifted into the cockpit. Several of Luke's classmates were also getting their planes ready. "How did I get myself into this?" Luke said to himself.

Just then he heard a familiar voice inside his head: *Trust in the Force, Luke.* It was the voice of his old friend and teacher, Ben Kenobi, a brave Jedi knight. Ben had trained Luke to use a special power called the Force. Luke had almost forgotten that. Now he jumped into his plane as Threepio waved farewell.

Then Luke and his crew of brave young pilots took off in the direction of the maverick moon.

As they neared the moon, a shrill screaming sound seemed to fill their ears. The fighter planes started to shake uncontrollably. Violent waves of color surrounded them. The magnetic field was so strong that not one of the planes could get through it.

The Force is with you! said the powerful voice inside Luke's head.

By themselves now, Luke and Artoo plunged on!

Suddenly Luke Skywalker broke through the magnetic field. He found himself in a shaky orbit around the maverick moon.

"Prepare to fire the Zukonium rays!" Luke shouted to Artoo. "We'll have to get out of here in a split second!"

The Zukonium rays were aimed at the center of the moon.
Luke squeezed down on the firing lever.

It was a direct hit! The impact of the exploding moon sent Luke's plane reeling out of control. Artoo's lights blinked on and off as his circuits blew.

Desperately Luke tried to regain control. But he didn't have to worry. The Force was with him. The special power he could not explain protected him and steered him free from danger.

When Luke and Artoo Detoo returned to
the hangar, the entire population of the Academy
was there to greet them with yells and cheers.
Happiest of all were their good friends
Princess Leia and See Threepio.

Princess Leia placed a medal of honor around Luke's neck. "Now we can get back to work," said Luke, feeling a little embarrassed.

"I'm glad that you and the Planetary Pioneers will be able to continue your work," said Leia. "But I'm even happier that you are alive and safe."